REDISCOVER
THE
POWER WITHIN

Learn to think positive.
Start believing in yourself & take control of your life.
Shape events around you & create a life of abundance

Ruchi

Pharos Books

ISBN: 978-93-5546-193-3
eISBN: 978-93-5546-201-5

©Publishers

Publisher: Pharos Books (P) Ltd.
Plot No.-55, Main Mother Dairy Road
Pandav Nagar, East Delhi-110092
Phone: 011-40395855
WhatsApp: +14049995474
E-mail: sales@pharosbooks.in
Website: www.pharosbooks.in
Edition: 2022

Rediscover the Power Within
Ruchi

Contents

CHAPTER 1

In this book, I would like to portray the entire picture of rediscovering the power within. I know, you are trying to identify and guess what you would be getting and how you would be benefited by reading this book. So, here we are!!! We, as human beings always focus on the benefits whether it is financial, emotional or else it could be in terms of learning, gaining knowledge, gaining experiences…so on and so forth. It is obvious because human minds are trained from childhood to do whatever brings you success in life. It has often been observed in children that as he goes ahead in life, as he grows and develops from a child to an adult, he develops a strong competitive behaviour and his mind gains this content unknowingly. Every child develops some unique traits and some common traits. When a child cries, he knows that in order to get the desired thing in life, he must use his power of convincing, if not by words, but by expression of crying. So, he shouts loudly and shouts so loudly that his parents listen to him and fulfils his wish, likewise he gains experience and uses this experience to get his wishes fulfilled each time. Lucky children…. how lucky they are, does that same rule apply to adults as well? You must be wondering how…. it's a fact that when an adult cries alone seeking God's support, he will definitely get it. When we wish for something, don't you think we become anxious and eager to get it fulfilled as soon as we can…don't you think the same rule applies as a solution to our problems and challenges and our desires…. like our parents, God first checks and decides whether this is the right time and right demand and by fulfilling it may not harm others.

Let us analyse another side of a common child….a child acquires knowledge, builds skills, learns and grasps the concepts taught in school not in order to enhance his calibre and to gain interest and happiness from studies, but in fact to satisfy his worldly desires, as it has been regularly fed in the minds of a kid that if he scores good marks, if he is better than the best, his success is counted not by the number of friends or the learnings he has gained and can share but by the result to calculate his success. In terms of growth of personality, a child who is able to secure marks may gain a sense of confidence as that is the beginning of people liking him, not because of his deeds and nature or behaviour, but rather by the success of his scores he is able to gain popularity and that satisfies even a child's ego, which can eventually make him egoistic to an extent that cannot be reverted. It becomes his innate quality to satisfy his ego with these small experiences in school.

Let us now uncover some other features of a child who does not know the meaning of fear, anxiety, sadness, depression and several other negative thoughts that are far apart from a kid who is just busy in his own world, uncovering the realities of life…even a fresh fruit or a vegetable taste is new for a child. He tries to distinguish the new tastes of real life with his senses. Ultimately, when a baby grows into an adult human being, he inculcates his experiences and incorporates those experiences to gain further new experiences in real and reel life ahead of him.

O

CHAPTER 2

—⊂ȝৎঌ—

Here, as we move on exploring life as a human being and with a keen desire to know about the philosophy of life and God, I would like to add that each individual is a pure soul. Each human being possesses the power of being a doer and with his capabilities which develops over a period of time can only be possible due to his survival *i.e.,* with the balance of mind, body and soul which each of us become what we conceive and what we want to achieve. The realisation of being an absolute human being is the ultimate truth of life. We must realise that we are not God however, we are as minute as an atom of God. Human beings are like an *'ansah'* of God and not God Himself. Being the minute part of God, we are also the creators, generators and destructors. Don't you think this is the ultimate thought? Human beings can generate, operate and destruct and make or break the universe with the power similar to God but not God himself. As we possess these ultimate sources of energy, we can create wonders in the world and of course history proves that human beings have always been creating masterpieces, he has been inventing, researching and utilising the creative power to generate such wonderful and unique creations. As such we must realise we own some powers but not the power as a whole… to change and transform the world according to our needs and definitely the ruling power of all is God.

As a child grows by observing his surroundings, he keeps an eye on the behaviour of his elders. He starts to crawl as he sees adults walk, he just wants to stand up and copy his parents, however, a child doesn't know his limitations. A child has no boundaries in mind. He just learns what he sees and listens. Let us try to understand it better—let us imagine a baby in a mother's womb, does he know what all he is going to learn and face once he grows, yet, time plays an important role and he grows unknowingly, without any signs of positive or negative traits. The baby is unaware of the traditions he will have to follow once he becomes a child, at different phases of the development he undergoes tremendous trials and tribulations which only that baby and the mother can experience. Ultimately, the baby gains a lot of courage to face these and as a result the baby closes his eyes and folds his hands very tightly. However, when he is forced by the doctors to see the world of fantasies, he cries in the beginning but then calms down as if he knows now that he needs to face it. With the burst of cry and ultimately the calmness does not it suggest that we need to be at peace with ourselves as we are born with a sense of accepting challenges. Now that the baby is an omen of peace and tranquility how can we think differentiating between a baby boy and a girl. But this is the fact of life and these facts are more dangerous thoughts then actions. Because difference of thoughts may lead to different actions which one may not even imagine. Another part of the reality is that each one of us has to face the reality and can't escape from this so-called biasness of gender.

Chapter 3

Now, let us focus on the very natural attitude of each individual. We have the tendency to admire our own deeds and actions what we call ego and another aspect what we call self-respect. We tend to forget that whatever we are, our thoughts, actions and decisions are controlled by a superpower. From the birth of a child till the death of a person, human beings think that he is the ultimate ruler and master of this universe, however, he is completely mistaken. He may think or overthink that he can create his destiny by his hard work or smart work, and may be the ruler of his fate, but unfortunately he has to give up once he gets surrounded by uncertain ambiguous situations and scenes which he may never have thought of. That's where the power of God is and he realises and surrenders to Him.

What do you think? There are many wonders of the world that has been created by humankind. However, is it right to take the whole credit by ourselves? Are we, human beings the creator of the world, the environment and nature? Are we the observer of nature or are we the destructor of the universe? Here is what a generic scenario is. Each individual be it man, woman or child or an adolescent child, all of us think that yes, we can do it. We live by our principles, thoughts and ideas. We try to give logic and reasoning to ourselves based on our past experiences and learnings from our school, college, job and business.

Don't you think we are just a puppet in the hands of nature. The universe in itself has immense power. Are we thinking beyond our minds and trying to rule over the universe? The ultimate source of power may lie in the generator, operator and destructor, we may also call it Brahma, Vishnu or Mahesh?

Then, who are we, why are we born, what's our purpose of birth and rebirth, what all tasks we need to do and what all results we would get? Human, this word in itself says, 'Hey u Man. Don't u think so?' Can humans do whatever they wish to? Are wishes granted? Whose whishes are granted and by whom, again a question mark? Yes, we as human beings think all our wishes could be granted by God or that power if we have full faith in Him…Isn't it true? On the other hand, we also think that God helps those who help themselves so, we can only have our wishes fulfilled if we take the right actions with the right decisions, however, don't you think whatever we decide is already pre-decided by God for us.

So, I am not God but, I am part of God or maybe a messenger of God. God is within us and we are all within Him. Yes, what I feel is, I am not God, God is in every cell yet, it is aloof of that cell. We can feel the presence but not the absence of God in every tiniest living beings. God has always given us power to think, act and to yield the results of our actions in terms of monetary gains, emotional well-being or physical wellness, and that makes results of our deeds and makes our destiny. In all, some part or situation is bound to happen but some things are part and parcel of our everyday actions, behaviour and even our thoughts which may lead to a better future or may even make our life miserable. So, ultimately it starts with thoughts, actions and later decisions which make our attitude which in turn becomes our habit and that leads to results which is definitely making our destiny. However, the ultimate truth is that after life it's death and the soul rests in

    Rediscover the Power Within

peace. With due course, our life, our destiny is the beginning and end which starts with our soul and ends with our soul. Now, here comes a question for all of us? Are we able to ever understand the truths and miracles of life or death or are we always to remain in a dilemma?

O

Let us be practical and logical, however, being spiritual never means that we are in some other world, that is impractical. We perceive what we see, we do what we perceive and the tasks that we do or the conclusions that we derive in our minds may make or break us from within. It's a real treasure and pleasure to understand the concepts of life, God and humans since they are all connected with each other in this universe. Now that we have explored the tiniest bit of life and its miracles, do we realise that God is always offering and offering us wholeheartedly, whether we complain or regret or even curse our own existence even when we are frustrated with our life. In fact, humans are the luckiest creation or creature on Earth. Who can ever think about his or her own luck and destiny, as if God has given him permission to change it according to his deeds? Can we pause here and at this very moment just see the surroundings and silently watch nature with our imagination soaring high. In this present moment, what the creation is, how the nature is, how wonderfully everything is aligned with time and everything seems to be pre-planned as if it has to be there, so it is. How selflessly the universe is giving us in abundance? So here what does abundance mean? Is it only the abundance of money, wealth and financial freedom? Can we really see in a broad sense what abundance is like? Is it abundance of thoughts, abundance of blessings, love, kindness generosity. The foremost of all is abundant energy, "urja" the "power." Humans have abundant power, whether it's in dormant stage or active state. Each of us possess significant characteristics. Each one is distinct from the other. "How Powerful?" Every leaf is different from the other in size, shape or colour. Likewise, each artery or vein may be different from the other inside our body with thousands of complexities. Every individual has been designed uniquely. Each one's thoughts, views and perspectives are different. Each one is different in physical, emotional and mental state. Even though we try to compare ourselves and doubt our capabilities by seeing others improving, every individual has different capabilities, however, the basic qualities remain the same. Although God made us alike yet, He kept these differences so that each one of us can admire his or her uniqueness and this uniqueness creates oneness or connection with God. How can we not pay our sincere gratitude towards that Power? The power who created us, who is maintaining our existence, keeping an eye on our every action and reaction and giving us fruits of our results in many forms. Shall we be thankful to God for our existence? Now, here is another perspective of life. We may think life is not so wonderful or not so rosy as it seems to be. However, this outlook of ours to feel and react negatively towards life and its tribulations is also part of our basic nature. We cannot ignore our negative traits as it is another side of the same coin which has to coexist in our thoughts. They rather make us cautious and aware of our negative impact which may otherwise happen. Don't you think had there been no negative nature how would we realise the value of positive and affirmative actions and reactions?

CHAPTER 5

—⊱⊰—

You may desire to be perfectly perfect with no negativity inside you. You are filled with all super positive thoughts and super powerful positive energy. However, when the sun rises it sets too, so if you are filled with anger at one thought you may be filled with compassion at another thought. We get sunshine and admire the bright light that brings positivity and enlightens ourselves, on the other side the sun sets at its own unique timings. So, every day is followed by every night. Light is followed by darkness and darkness again changes to light the next day. It's an inevitable cycle that continues. We can never imagine how and why this cycle is so crucial and beyond our imagination. We are getting the ultimate power in the form of energy we own. So, light has its own power of positivity and darkness has its own power or calmness, it's how we perceive. At night, darkness becomes powerful by the beautiful moonlit and starts shining in a wonderful fashion, will it not become boring and dull if we receive only sunshine and no night view which may have inspired many writers to write poetry. Limelight comes with darkness, and after experiences of failure, one is bound to achieve threads of success. At night, plants release carbon dioxide and humans regain energy by sleeping at night, liberating all tensions and stress to have a good night's sleep in order to rejuvenate himself and to move ahead achieving the next level of success next day. And thus, he is full of energy and vitality with full enthusiasm and is ready to face the world again. So, my question to you is why do we not accept negative behaviour of others or even if it is ours. Once we start accepting the faults of others and ourselves, we would never complain. How positive one may feel after he is done with releasing his anger in the form of acceptance and forgiveness instead of shouting on top of his voice. Even after crying we feel relieved from stress as if negative energy has been burnt rather washed away in the tears. This is how negative energy gets its way out. To fill in the positive energy within ourselves are we not pondering everywhere, even then we may say we come back to zero and ultimate zero. I would give you the key of happiness here, remain neutral that is, don't get excited or too much happy when you gain positive experience and neither full of sad emotions when negative thoughts or events surround you. Its ultimate happiness *i.e.*, inner happiness lies when you see yourself beyond happiness and sadness. That is when you feel calmness and extreme peace within you and your thoughts.

Don't you think that success comes with a positive attitude? A positive mindset can only bring positive actions and positive actions can yield positive outcomes and once these outcomes become our habit, positive changes comes easily as the negative ones. Do you agree or disagree? We may be in a state of dilemma now, how can positivity prolong and last longer and overrule negativity. So here comes the solution for this "change happens in a moment." Yes, its rightly stated. Positive and negative are two sides of the same human being just like the front and back side of a human body? It's the two sides of the same human mindset. In fact, it's inseparable from each other. It's an illusion which we have created for ourselves, in fact, it's a myth. I must say a virtual thing like a virtual memory of a computer is our subconscious mind. Can we see or touch these negative or positive thoughts, you may wonder how is it that these energies exist? Only we can see the positive and negative images or events if we want to imagine positive or negative, we may think from that angle and as we think deeper these thoughts gain consistency. So, these images are nothing but the words and words are nothing but vibrations so let's unfold the mystery that it's all vibration that we can feel within our surroundings. Why do we feel calmness when we enter any temple or mosque, its only because of chanting they do, the positive energy that vibrate in those areas which ultimately are caught by the fellow persons who worship there? So ultimately the words may carry an image and we cannot say for sure that images came first or language *i.e.*, words and images are the origin of vibrations. However, we know that language forms an integral part of the universe.

Chapter 6

I would like you to think over and over again something negative and then positive. Do you get images or words in your mind? Just analyse your thoughts. Don't you think while a child is taught any language, he or she is asked to see the image and then along with it is the letter or word. Every word has a meaning either in the form of an image or in the form of abstract or virtual feelings. Some words capture the innate quality of human beings and thus when a person always talks politely his nature becomes vibrant. On the other hand, if anyone uses abusive language, his character becomes like that of a demon. So, no one is born as God or a Demon, it's the quality we inculcate while being in the society, in our day-to-day activities and thoughts. We take or make decisions based on these negative and positive thoughts and based on our intellectual abilities to analyse and judge. The better logical thinking power we have, the better it helps us to take the right decisions at the right time. So ultimately, we need to analyse both positive and negative aspects of an image with the words attached to it that give it a meaning.

Now we would like to take it deeper, does images have the power or the words or the sounds and vibrations? Let us answer this. We are here to think logically, however, our mind, body and soul may not be that capable of identifying this mystery of the universe.

The more I tried to analyse, the more life and its folds kept on asking me questions. The more you dig deeper the more freshwater you get. The more you do brainstorming of your mind, the more capable you become. Let us take an activity for ourselves to analyse our lives and challenges and try to find solutions to our problems, however, we really limit

 Rediscover the Power Within

ourselves be it financially, be it related to our health or physique, be it psychological, emotional or relationship challenges. Many of us think alike. Don't you feel that there are some common thoughts, some common problems, some common tasks, some common problem-solving techniques we all utilise to make our lives easy and simple. It depends on how each of us really become limitless or do we keep struggling with our challenges of life. Let me give an example:

A mathematical problem has a solution that already exists, even then the student needs to mention each and every step to reach the solution. There may be a common solution, an unique solution or many ways to solve the same problem. However, it depends on the students' intellect or an individual what all steps he takes to reach the heights of success by utilising his capability to put forth the right foot forward and to get the right decision at the right time. In addition, a mathematical problem demands accuracy and speed of calculation determines the efficiency and the right solution is achieved if the student follows rules and guidelines laid by mathematicians *i.e.,* the formulas. We can relate this to our life's success, we need to follow guidelines and be at pace with times to achieve our aim of life.

CHAPTER 7

—⚬—

``How we start decides what our end result will be.''

I would now like to take you on a tour of my strategy of problem-solving. I would like to disclose my way of problem- solving, to finding solutions to my challenges of life. Maybe you find it interesting to implement and you would like to follow but its solely your decision. You should not follow these steps if you don't believe it or else if you can substantiate it with a better way of dealing with life's complicated situations.

Starting with—devote your 100%-time energy and focus on solving the challenges. Begin by analysing it's all aspects thoroughly by writing it down in your own words. It could be that your mind is full of words and confusion overwhelms you. However, when you start putting your thoughts, your thought process starts streamlining while you put each thought into words. Because thoughts may be jumbled up but logically you can't jumble up words. This exercise will make you feel better and bitter both but just have faith that you are going to get a unique solution, trust yourself and the Power, the universal power that whatever you are facing is for the time being and it will soon pass by, however finding solutions at present makes a person so much anxious that he loses the focus on the solution and rather keeps on rethinking about the problem description.

Can we think—or find a way or make a way. It is my life and I am going to deal with it, no matter what the solution is and that's the possible outcome of my efforts. No one else is going to solve my problems better than myself as I am determined to do so. Why would even anyone else be bothered and responsible for my problems and solutions. Everyone has his or her own share of problems. Just like set A and B of a question paper, every candidate has to complete his or her answer sheet based on the given different set of questions. Once you analyse it, picturise it in your mind and have it written in words, I would say 70% task is done. Now as you are writing, you would certainly feel that you have the power and energy to solve it. You may get different answers to the same problems however, once you filter out the right solutions, you are a winner by yourself, yes, you are…don't you think so? So many small problems if you are able to solve by this easy method, I am sure small problems will go away from your life and you now know how to deal with as many small problems you may face at any time. I am sure you would challenge yourself and enjoy solving problems instead of cursing your life why this problem and why that problem, because now you know the logical problem-solving method. And do you think problems may be bigger than your level? I would say at each stage of life you get problems to solve, that would be of your level, within your limits and within your level of understanding. Once you cross the hurdles of problems you may now focus on solutions… However, if you think that this problem has no solution then I would say just train your mind to admit that no solution means no value, that means your problem has no value that's why it has no solution. There will always be contradictions and you don't have to get engulfed in that. If you don't have any solution then realise this is nothing but a problem which doesn't need my attention. So, the next step is to just free your mind and with this surrender yourself and your thoughts to God ultimately whether you have a solution or whether there is no solution and no problem, all will be taken care of by the Ultimate Power and the Ultimate Universe. Because once you surrender, you are getting connected with God or with that power, when you keep on struggling with your own, then Power doesn't play its role, it simply lets you go. So, decide and let go…

Chapter 8

❦

When you think and analyse that only you have the power then God thinks and lets him solve his problem. In fact, God has made us capable of solving each and every problem that exists. There could be 3 types of solutions depending upon the problem. It could be **No solution, Unique solution or Infinitely many solutions**. The same applies to challenges of our life. When we are facing the problem, we usually try to look at the problem from different angles, however, never try to solve the problem with focus and by drawing conclusion from the problem itself. In fact, we should consider ourselves aloof of problems or challenges and suggest ourselves the solution just as if we are trying to solve our friend's problem.

Once we become an audience of our problem or you can say we become the spectator of our problem we can analyse from different angles and gain better perspective of our solution. We may become solution-oriented instead of problem-oriented. And in this way the process of solving problem becomes easier so much so that we may start applying the solutions with joy and may even explore things at a deeper level. We may apply all our logics and principles or so-called notions and beliefs and come up with a firm resolution or conclusion that relives our tensions. Now, that our attitude is of solution-giver rather than solution-seeker, we may get tempted to accept challenges head on. Moreover, we may start taking the responsibility of our decisions. As each of us whether of any age has to be responsible for our thoughts, actions, beliefs and decisions.

Can we now change the perspective of being solution-oriented and try to focus on certain magical things? Yes, you read it right, magic. Life starts with magic and ends in magic and life revolves magically around us by giving us so much that we never dreamt of or may be our wishes came true magically while being alive and completely in tune with ourselves.

Here, I would like to share some wonderful learnings that helped many people to create wonders in life. The magic starts in your life once you really wish for it and believe in it, and once you start visualising the magic miracles start pouring into your life as easily as you start believing in them. The foremost part of one's life is *'sangat adat'* and *'Guru'* - these are crucial aspects that one should always seek in order to achieve success as these are basic guidelines or pathways to success. These are the 3 Pillars or foundations of one's life. Life is a mystery and we keep on unfolding it and really, we need the right company or the right companion at the right time to solve our problems.

The first pillar is 'Sangat' or 'Company' or 'Community'. As we all agree, a person is known by the kind of people he belongs to and is judged by his deeds. If a child grows in the company of studious friends he develops the learning attitude, however if the same child by mistake gets into wrong or bad company like if he makes his friendship with children who lack focus in studies but takes interest in wrong deeds like stealing, drinking, etc. the child automatically gains this bad tendency and his thoughts and actions become out of control of even his parents. So, we should be very careful while choosing our company. If you want to be a successful businessman or an entrepreneur or CEO, try to find the company of such people. Try to forcefully think like founders so that wherever you go you meet like-minded people. If you want to be healthy, find the company of people who maintain their diet strictly and follow a strict exercise routine.

The second pillar 'Adat' or 'Habit' is even all the more important as 'Sangat'. It takes 90:90:1 rule to develop a habit that means 90 continuous days for 90 minutes of daily practice of 1 thing, focus on one thing that you want to be your habit. It definitely takes time to build and rebuild a habit, however that is not impossible. There's no age factor involved. So, let's not give an excuse but start developing good habits day-by-day keeping our focus be it as simple as exercise, or be it diet control. Drinking lots of water, eating healthy food, reading books, inculcating learning habits be it so simple as sleeping less and working more it just takes an effort to become what you want to be. Once you decide your path of journey then destination doesn't seem so far. When you become constantly aware of your habits and your efforts you gain the right attitude and momentum. You gain the right kind of perspective and thought process becomes so simplified and focused those actions give tremendous results. Once you start achieving

 Rediscover the Power Within

results the thirst of achieving more and more lets you to become a successful human being on earth.

I must now reveal the third and the most strongest pillar. 'Guru' or 'Mentor' is the ultimate edifice behind the success of any individual. Some people just ignore the fact that Guru can only show you the path, can show you the right direction and those who ignore this fact and do not seek guidance of guru success ignores them. So, for some people guidance of the guru is like the second nature of God that guides them. Guru shows the path of ultimate happiness and always wishes that his **shishya** or mentee may become more learned than him. So, *'Guru gur, Chela shakkar'*…we all have heard of this quote. *Sanidhya* of Guru is important as Guru shows you the way, helps you in identifying your vision, purpose of life. Guide or Guru walks with you when people may throw stones at you. He may guide you to collect the stones and make a temple of those stones or make a path of your own with those stones. So, here's the positivity of thought that comes into play. Guru gives us ATM Gyan whenever we get diverted, Guru brings us back on the right track.

These three pillars are of utmost importance in life as we can realize life's important principles and always following these 3 rules of 'sangat adat' and 'Guru' can bring an ultimate change in our lives and also give us inner peace and happiness which we always desire for.

CHAPTER 9

Now, we would be exploring life further and moving towards the achievement of our goals. Let us learn and implement the way of creating miracles, yes, we can create miracles. You read it rightly, but you may wonder how. So, there's an art and science of creating miracles in life. To simplify a miraculous word "Miracle" let's just learn this art of fulfilling miracles.

We, as the creator of miracles can actually visualise, vocalise and emotionalise to actualise the greatest and almost every wish of ours. Whatever we can think of and describe, using it in the right sense with utmost feeling of strength and confidence and having full faith in ourselves and God, we can eventually make it into a reality.

So let's say my target is, I want to achieve my goal of selling 110 million copies of my book so I will visualise that I have really achieved my goal, sold 110 million copies and now celebrating this event of happiness with my friends and family on a specific date say on my birthday. Then, I will put more efforts into it and start vocalising it, declaring it to the world, so that the whole universe gets aligned to my thoughts and make it come true. I can make it pubic through social media groups and to my family members so that actually to keep my words I will act with all my strength and focus to accomplish the goal. Surely, I will start feeling that my success is on my way or I am on my way to fulfilment of my success. So, while writing the book, I will put all my focus and attention in adding value to the content which I may deliver to my readers so that it becomes a bestseller and ultimately

 Rediscover the Power Within

the readers will eventually make my book a big hit.

Formula for Actual Miracles to Happen in Life ➜ **V + V + E = Am (Visualise + Vocalise + Emotionalise = Actualise).**

Now, this formula demands certain commitment that is ZERO Doubt and 100% Action.

Look and apply these 11 principles or golden rules of Visualisation.

1. Visualise end result.

2. Never ask how it will happen.

3. Visualise it, believe it and forget it.

4. Do not be desperate.

5. Do it at least once in a day and a number of times.

6. Do it at the same time daily.

7. Fix your place to do visualisation.

8. Do the manifestation mudra.

9. Keep smiling while visualising as if your goals have been accomplished.

10. Do it with a smile and face north for materialistic goals.

11. Do It with a positive intention.

So, we can write down 108 intentions and as there's power of intention and visualisation that we must realise and take benefit of. As is said, "Everything is Co-Creation, Nothing is Coincidence." Where logic stops magic begins….

Let us now take action, become a director of our own life and write a script and let it play over the whole night daily and we can definitely decode the universe signals while we are asleep.

Chapter 10

Let us now unfold another important aspect of life. We may say that the ultimate crux of life is to maintain a balance between health, wealth and relationship. So, this is like a vicious cycle. It's like a triangle with 3 sides equal. We may add our own theories and principles and even work on those pre-built principles to gain and attain equilibrium between health, money and relationship challenges.

Let us begin with some basic concepts and understanding of how we can do purification of space, body and relationship.

We need to clear the clutter in our houses, just get rid of old clothes, machinery, grocery, devices or any other junk items from your home to remove negativity. This will clean the space and make you feel light and relaxed as you may feel less burdened to maintain it and by giving it to the poor may bring a sense of satisfaction to your own self. We may clean and clear our cupboards, kitchenware can be nicely cleaned and placed systematically so that each item becomes easily accessible. This reduces our time and effort to find items when required and thus gives us a sense of cleanliness and thus maintains our hygiene.

Next, we can start cleansing our body and mind by devoting 90 minutes daily to meditate, exercise and feed our mind everyday with books of motivation and enriching our life with biographies of successful people, devote 1000 times of hard work towards taking action for our goals and mission. Once we have clarity of thoughts our body is fit, mind is very calm and well prepared to lead a happy life without any resentment. And the best part is that once we gain achievements in our lives, relationships and challenges comes with a solution on its own as a bonus gift. Because once a person is financially strong, mentally balanced and emotionally powerful we can deal with relationship aspects quite sensibly. We need to nurture our relationships, our bonding with our family and friends with care and show gratitude towards each bond we make with any human being.

Other basic rules of life could be to master the pain and pleasures of life. As every desire comes with a pain so every desire is bounded by God's wish. So, pain and pleasure feelings can go together. We need to be neutral towards every aspect of life. Just be a viewer, a spectator of life and not an interferer of God's wish and God may offer you in abundance.

In all, let's just visualise our power in coordination with God and work towards God's purpose and align our thoughts and actions in favour of universal intentions. Once our intentions match with that of the universe, we start creating miracles and this magical feeling can be marvelous. The universe can be wholeheartedly helping us in terms of achieving our mission, and thus we can do wonders in life, we may seek universal guidance and can go beyond our expectations. This can bring inner peace and satisfaction not only in our lives but in every individual who comes in contact with us and can become enlightened with our companionship.

Another aspect, I may like to describe is learning how to manage rejection, frustration, fears and financial pressure. By paying gratitude to the abundant nature we have, we can be free of these negative thoughts that can damage our life beyond any measure. We must be thankful for whatever tangible and intangible things we have acquired and by God's grace we are breathing in this world, being alive and thankfully able to work towards our greatest mission whatever it may be. Every one may be given all or at least one quality better then the rest, which makes him unique. We must identify our strengths and our weaknesses in order to achieve our purpose of life, only earning and yearning for materialistic things does not make us the master of the universe, we must always seek what we have been born for, our ultimate achievement of life is in realization of ourselves. It's not that anyone can reject and frustrate us until we give him permission to do so. We must be in full control of our senses and our deeds that no one can ideally misuse our company be it financially or emotionally.

Let us look at another learning *i.e.*, creators never complain and complainers never create. This thought may be a random thought but it is really valuable as it helps us understand human nature. So those individuals who always complain can never seek the creation, because most of their time, effort and emotions goes in complaining rather than thinking of creating anything useful for the world? On the other hand, the creators are the rulers as they never complain and just devote full time and energy, to complete their focus in solving the problem and innovating. So, as an individual we should never complain that the system is corrupt, we can't change it, we cannot do anything about it, instead raise ourselves to the realization that every individual has the capability to be a creator, because we all have originated from the same creator, the ultimate power, God. We should embrace our good qualities and just deviate from wrong deeds and focus on creating the solutions. To every problem there's a solution, if any problem has no solution, then it's not a problem anymore. It's as simple as that.

CHAPTER 11

I would like to share some more learnings with you…

Repetition is the mother of all learning, and implementation is the father of all learnings.

Zig Ziglar says, "Repetition is the mother of learning, the father of action, which makes it the architect of accomplishment."

Now that we are fully motivated and want to change the world and become the most powerful person….let's begin to practice these learnings. Here lies the tricks…

Do you really want to know about tricks and trips. Read on and on. Read more books not only this…and yes practice, practice and practice….

The way to become a champion is to practice a lot, do repetitions with dedication with full faith in yourself. I am sure that sincere efforts pay in the long run, be it in any form, the more you practice, the more you are on your way to perfectionism. We don't practice to become perfect because no one can attain or be perfect yet, we can do things in a way that leads beyond perfection just by being consistent in practicing. Practicing with a focused mindset is what can bring results.

Let's make it simpler, just being consistent and focused is the key to all success stories, you can even judge yourself once you are focused and consistent in anything and once you start getting results you feel more confident while practicing and that what makes your efforts more result-oriented. So, what are you waiting for, keep your routine on track, have no mercy on yourself and start focused learning and practicing consistently

 Rediscover the Power Within

because you have that power, that power lies within you and within the universe that's going to support your mission? So, make a SMART (Specific, Measurable, Achievable, Realistic and Timely) goal and just get started and as you know well begun is half done.

Now, that we are a step ahead in learning and implementation, I hope you must be wondering what's in it for me. So my friends, young or adult readers ....I must say that there is a lot to learn, lot to practice and lot to implement, however don't you agree how we find it difficult to manage it all. I know almost 90% of us struggle with time management syndrome ie., How to manage time for all these things whatever goals we make but time is limited we may think.

But, I may suggest to you in this virtual world of thoughts, words, feelings and now virtuality in actions through robots, let's see Time as a virtual thing as well. Let's look at it this way, we may know that the sun rises in the East, but there is a contradiction that sun is a start and earth revolves around it, so how can we admit that sun is rising and setting? How can we admit the fact that the clock that we follow is real. Not to hurt anyone's assumptions, but I want to portray in earlier days when there was no time system and no clock people use to work according to paher like morning, afternoon and evening.

Why do we keep worrying that a day has passed and another day and yet another day, without accomplishment of results...?

Why can't we think that whatever we are destined to do we are on our path of doing it. The actions we are taking are already destined, like some of us believe in past karma which makes us work the way we are in the present. So, our present karma or the present tasks are already pre-decided by the universe. We are not God, but yes, we all have a part of God's nature. Can't we think positively that whatever lifetime we have we just need to work according to our thoughts. And why thoughts because our minds are connected to God's second nature. That's the ruling power we have. Have you ever thought how thoughts generate, how thoughts create actions and how actions bring results? Don't you think it's all miraculously integrated by God's will? The ultimate power within us may be God's nature, so we may corelate our nature with God.

Even I think I am writing, because I have been destined to write, my purpose may be anything and my goal and my mission may be anything. But I am writing this book, may be because God may have destined my duty and my karma may have formed this scene and that I am creating thoughts…in fact God may be ruling my mind and asking me to write these thoughts and make people aware of their inner strengths and weaknesses. Some people may even doubt this. However, one person who wants to see negative sense will always find negatives and another person who is curious to find positive sense may be filled with intense positivity. It depends on an individual and his or her thoughts where he or she could explore their imagination to. Can we now say our beliefs shape our destiny…I hope we may link these learnings and do something fruitful?

Another Important aspect I may like to share here with you is related to the above concept. We must become aware of our belief system…Ask why we should get rid of this negative belief because once you have figured out your negative beliefs and the trauma of that then only you will start to accept the positive belief. Think about new beliefs which you want to achieve, visualise your positive beliefs and you may gain an universal support in fulfilling that.

Chapter 12

—⊸⊰⊱⊸—

Now that we have accepted the positive belief system, we can keep on repeating the process of learning and practicing till we become fully convinced by our belief system that old negative beliefs are gone and we are leading a new powerful life.

Let's work on these learnings too.

Do we have…a growth mindset?

Have we…a fixed mindset?

So, do we and have …means we should be with a mindset with whatever we have and do and take actions accordingly and then we may seek positive results. If we keep on waiting for the right time and right set of facilities or right direction and just sit and watch…we may never reach our goal. So just start with whatever you have and do whatever you can.

Everything that happens is the best possible thing that could ever happen and we may improve it joyfully.

We may think that it's not the right thing or we may feel that I am facing all problems but don't we all feel happy once we overcome the problems of our lives. *Life hai to problems hain, death ke sath to sab problems hi khatam* so the choice is not ours but it's God's wish to keep us engaged in problems so that we may be alive and keep solving the challenges accepting them till eternity and making this world better and better.

If you do not get what you want you may get something better…So, it's not our wish that whatever results even in the form of happiness or struggles we may face, all we have to deal with ourselves. We may remain focused on whatever we have and feel happiness by paying gratitude or else we may choose to crib always and repent by being sad and unhappy of our results. Don't you think we have that power; we may imagine that we are happy and may become happy at one moment and if we feel that we are going to be sad feelings of frustration start creeping into our thoughts. So, let's utilise our power in a positive way whichever way we can think of.

———— ☙❦ ————

Chapter 13

Pain is just power wrapped in puzzles and every game is winnable if you play it big enough… and every action is easy if you make it small enough…

Evolution is smooth as you are humble and joy is accessible as you are faithful.

There can be so many learnings to know that we have the power…the power within, but the realization of the fact can make us more powerful. If you think your power is in your mind you can definitely focus on improving your skills based on your inner instinct. You may think that you are more capable in terms of playing game, enhance your skills in playing game by practicing hard. You may be keen to follow the path of salvation and want to achieve the enlightenment …so why not go ahead in practicing that. Why are we so much bothered about consequences even before taking the first step…its just like a toddler is very fearful of putting that first step forward but believe me …once you overcome that challenge all other challenges on your way is just like a cake walk…

However, some of us may still be in confusion that all this is theoretically correct but what's practical is that we all have to face challenges, we need money not only to survive but to fulfill our worldly desires. So here my friends, why to worry…

Get started with whatever you have, whatever little is just enough to get started. It may take a long way or even a shortest way, you need to figure out with your own self, no one is going to guide you in this whole life journey. Yes, parents, relatives or friends anyone would not burn their finger to tell you that the fire is hot, you may have to figure it out on your own.

The best learning for me and may be for you is to find a way or make a way…and If you believe you can, You Can…Keeping these thoughts in mind and feeling the power of thoughts in actions by our physical self being motivated to achieve the desired results our soul may be actively listening to these thoughts and deeds. Let's do it and do it now…Change happens in a moment, so I would close this short and crisp learnings by saying, "Let the world talk about us and until it so happens let's not bother about the world, instead be focused and consistent to make our dreams come true."

9 789355 461933